DAVE KEANE

Joe Sherlock

KID DETECTIVE

Case #000002:

The Neighborhood Stink

HarperCollinsPublishers

Joe Sherlock, Kid Detective, Case #000002:
The Neighborhood Stink
Copyright © 2006 by David J. Keane

Library of Congress Cataloging-in-Publication Data
Keane, David, date
   The neighborhood stink / by David Keane.— 1st ed.
      p.   cm.— (Joe Sherlock, kid detective ; #000002)
   Summary: A super-sleuth fourth grader solves the case of
mysterious dog poop on his neighbor's front lawn.
   ISBN-10: 0-06-076187-3 (trade bdg.)
   ISBN-13: 978-0-06-076187-5 (trade bdg.)
   ISBN-10: 0-06-076186-5 (pbk. bdg.)
   ISBN-13: 978-0-06-076186-8 (pbk. bdg.)
   [1. Dogs—Fiction. 2. Neighbors—Fiction. 3. Mystery and
detective stories.] I. Title.
PZ7.K2172Cas 2006   2005014899
[Fic]—dc22   CIP
                                                  AC

Typography by Christopher Stengel
1 2 3 4 5 6 7 8 9 10
❖
First Edition

For Paris, Jade, and Sutter,
my Baker Street Irregulars
—D.K.

Contents

My name is Joe Sherlock.

But everyone calls me Sherlock, even my own parents. It sounds crazy, but my little sister didn't know my first name was Joe until she was almost six years old.

Of course, it makes perfect sense that I would be called Sherlock.

Why? Well, there's a bunch of old books written about a guy named Sherlock Holmes

1

who smoked a pipe, wore a creepy hat, and solved mysteries like nobody's business. I've never read any of them. But I've seen lots of movies about him. So he's kind of like my hero. We almost have the same name—except for the Joe and Holmes parts. And like the great Sherlock Holmes, I was born with a natural gift for solving mysteries.

Some kids my age can play the piano, break a board with a karate chop, or remember to make their beds every day. Not me. Not even close. But I can find just about anything that's lost. I can figure out the answer to a riddle way before grown-ups can. And I just love a good mystery.

But don't get the wrong idea. I'm no brain. In fact, I'm pretty crummy at school. Miss Piffle, my teacher, once told my parents at back-to-school night that I was "a bit daffy," which is basically a nice way of saying "Your

kid's a dope." But that's okay with me. I was born with a gift.

Sometimes I get a little help from my little sister, Hailey, who is sort of like my assistant. Actually, she's a bit of a troublemaker, so I have to make sure she doesn't play in the kitty litter or drop Dad's golf balls into the garbage disposal. She tags along sometimes. To be honest, sometimes she sees things that I miss . . . but mostly that's because she's a lot shorter than I am.

Anyway, before you start snoring like a banshee, I'd like you to sit back, relax, and watch your step as we plunge into my second official case as a private detective: Case #000002.

• Chapter Two •
Something Stinks

I'm in my room watching a Sherlock Holmes movie when I hear a knock on our front door.

"Is your son, Sherlock, at home?" I hear our neighbor Mrs. Fefferland ask my mom.

"He is, Mrs. Fefferland," my mom answers. "Please come in."

Mrs. Fefferland lives across the street from us. Her husband travels around the world selling plastic sprockets, gears, and other junk to people who need that kind of stuff. So Mrs. Fefferland has lots of free time to work in her yard, a well-clipped work of art that's surrounded by a white picket fence and off-limits to everyone.

"Did Sherlock break one of your windows again?" my mom asks.

Already my heart is thumping in my chest. Not because I think I might have my second official case, but because I never knew that Mrs. Fefferland knew I broke her kitchen window. Geez, that was like eighty decades ago, and my mom is still bringing it up!

"Nothing like that," Mrs. Fefferland says. "It's just that there's been some mysterious poop on my gated front lawn the past few days."

"You think Sherlock is pooping in your yard?" my mom gasps.

Now I'm ready to barf. My head starts

spinning. I'm ready to run out the back door and never come back . . . until I hear Mrs. Fefferland say, "Oh, no, dear. I just want to figure out whose dog is responsible. I want it cleaned up! Your Sherlock has a reputation in this neighborhood as a problem solver. I'm hoping he can help me catch that mystery mutt."

Whew! I thought I was being accused of being the Mad Pooper . . . but now I know it's just a mystery that needs solving. And like I said, I love a good mystery.

Mrs. Fefferland wheezes like a bath toy when she breathes and makes loud clacking noises with her teeth. Maybe after I solve her poop mystery, she'll let me figure out what's making all that racket in her mouth. But for the moment, I concentrate on the interview.

"Good afternoon, Mrs. Fefferland. What seems to be the trouble?" I ask, trying my best to sound like Sherlock Holmes.

"I've got a mystery pooper, and I want the culprit caught!" she wheezes and clacks.

"Interesting," I say, because I'm not sure what else to say. I wait for her to add something else, but she only fills the awkward silence with a steady, gurgling wheeze.

"Maybe it's your own dog, Mrs. Fefferland," I say with a shrug. "Could Tinker be the one pooping in your yard?"

The moment I say this, I know it's a mistake. Mrs. Fefferland looks at me like I just reached down her throat and pulled out a rubber duck.

"Of c-course n-not," she stammers. "Tinker . . . Tinker is never allowed in my front yard. Only the backyard. I'm the only one who is allowed in that yard!"

"Okay," I croak. "I'd like to get to the bottom of this mystery for you. My fee is ten dollars a day . . . plus expenses."

"Very well. I'd like you to get started right away," she says, standing up. "I'd like this unpleasant situation resolved by this evening."

"Certainly," I say, although I'm really thinking that I can't believe she said yes to ten bucks. "I'll be over in a few minutes."

"I'll be waiting," Mrs. Fefferland clacks. I close the door as she rumbles down the porch steps like a runaway piano.

"The game is afoot," I whisper—although I have no idea what that means; it was something Mr. Sherlock Holmes always said when he got a new case.

Tinker
backyard dweller only!

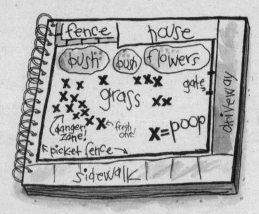

"This looks like a poop farm," exclaims my little sister.

"Thanks for that keen observation, Hailey," I murmur. Mrs. Fefferland has just waddled into her house, wringing her hands and clacking away about catching the bandit that's polluting her lawn. And I must admit, if you could see beyond the dog poops, her lawn was

an amazing accomplishment—like a smooth, green carpet.

"I need to make a map of the evidence field," I say, pulling out my sketch pad.

"Oh, like a treasure map for flies?" my sister giggles.

If you haven't already noticed, my little sister, Hailey, has an amazing talent for driving me insane.

"Well, like it or not, Hailey, this is evidence," I explain. "The orderly collection of evidence is a key skill of the successful detective."

"It looks like you've already collected some evidence on the bottom of your shoe," she says, and begins laughing as loud as an opera singer.

"Oh, that's a fresh one!" I gag, trying my best not to hurl on Mrs. Fefferland's beautiful lawn.

"Oh my gosh . . . that is so gross!" Hailey manages to squeeze in between giggles and snorts, fully enjoying the first misstep of my investigation.

"Hailey, just go home and get me another pair of shoes," I growl between clenched teeth.

"Yes, sir, Mr. Great Detective!" she says while saluting. Then she runs back across the street and into our house shouting, "Poop alert! Poop alert!"

That's when I make my first discovery in the case: All the evidence looks like it came from a small dog, but the fence around this yard is almost three feet high and would be difficult for a small dog to jump over. "The game is certainly afoot," I whisper as I scrape the bottom of my shoe on the curb.

"How about these, Sherlock?" Hailey screams from our front door. She flings her old pair of lavender ballet slippers onto our front steps. She squeals in delight and slams the door with a bang so loud that my teeth loosen.

"That's some assistant," I say, shaking my head.

"What do you know about dog poop?" I ask my older sister, Jessie, as she scribbles away at her homework.

I should mention here that not every decision a young detective makes is the right one. One decision I should have skipped was seeking help from friends and family.

"Wha'?" Jessie huffs. She looks at me with her mouth open and her eyes partially rolled back in her head. I'm never sure what this look means, especially since she makes this face no matter what's happening around her. "Oh, it's the turd nerd," she finally moans. "Mom told me all about your big case, and if you tell anyone at school, I'll kill you. Now get out, Inspector Dork."

"Thanks for all your love and support," I say as I shut her door. Saying something nice when you really mean something nasty is called sarcasm. My best friend, Lance Peeker, taught me this trick, and it drives Jessie crazy.

My next mistake is asking my mom for help. My mom baby-sits houseplants for people. She operates her business out of our living room, which is always filled with strange plants from around the neighborhood. She talks to these plants, which really spooks Lance whenever he comes over.

"Mom, have you seen any strange dogs lately?" I ask. She's on the phone with a nervous owner of a sickly orchid. As she talks, she starts spraying my hair with her mister bottle and using her fingers to comb my hair into my dad's goofy hairstyle. Now I look more like a nervous elf than a private detective. I exit quickly.

I find my dad catching up on his paperwork at the kitchen table. He's a quality assurance engineer, which is a fancy way of saying he shuffles papers around his desk all day. Sometimes these papers even shuffle all the way onto our kitchen table.

"Dad, what's your experience with dog poop?" I ask in an official voice.

After staring at me for a long time, he says, "Sherlock, have you given any thought to joining a sports team? Fresh air and exercise might be good for you."

"Oh, just forget it," I mumble.

When my mom hangs up the phone, I call Lance to see if he can come over and help with the case.

"No, thanks," says Lance. "I have to watch TV."

"You don't have to watch TV, Lance," I say. "You can come over now and watch TV later, after we solve the case."

"Well, I have to watch this educational show about flying squirrels with my grandma before I can play a video game," Lance says very slowly, because he's watching the flying squirrel show while we're talking.

"Thanks for helping me out, friend," I say.

"Hey, you're getting good at that sarcasm stuff," he says. "Grandma, did you see that crazy squirrel miss the tree? Uh . . . see ya, Sherlock."

"Bye," I say, hanging up the phone. Lance is my best friend, but he is extremely lazy for someone his age.

When I notice Hailey watching the same show about soaring tree squirrels, I sigh like a train that's come to a complete stop and squirts out steam. "This is something I must do alone," I say to no one in particular. Before I head out the front door, I do the single most important thing a detective must do to solve a crime. . . .

• Chapter Six •
The Unusual Suspects

In detective movies, the main guy always writes up a list of people he suspects could have done the crime. Then he keeps scratching names off the list one by one. This is a good idea because it helps everybody watching the movie to start guessing who did it.

I create my first list of suspects by simply making a list of the neighborhood dogs.

I look over my list until I'm satisfied that

Something Stinks!

Possible Poopers

Ranger: Grrr! The Castro's dog is as big as a house and as loud as thunder.

Peekaboo: Who ME? Looks like a freezing rat. Eyes 8 sizes too big for its head.

Vader: Arf! Old. Very Old! Older than rocks! Very unlikely he'd have energy for a poop n' run!!!!

Cujo: dog beard! The Ashers' new dog comes from the country that invented vampires! Bigger than a buffalo

Fred: Maybe the worst name for a dog ever! This dog never barks.

Smokey: The Sheldons' dog runs away several times a week. Smokey the Pooping Bandit!? Splash down

Ted: The second worst name I ever heard for a dog. Smooshed-up face looks like it got hit with a frying pan. Bang

these are all the suspects. I'm feeling better already, but time is slipping away. If I can nab the mystery doo-doo dog before dinner, I'll be ten bucks richer by bedtime.

"Take a good look at this," I say, handing Mr. Castro an instant photo of a fresh pile of evidence. "Take your time," I say, watching his face carefully for any signs of guilt. He stands in his doorway with a weird look on his face.

I borrowed (without asking, of course) Hailey's Girl Chat Sleepover instant camera and snapped a few good pictures of the evidence.

Her camera is pink and covered with flower stickers, but it sure spit out some good photographs. (I figured photos would work better than trying to scoop poop into a plastic bag.) A good detective must always preserve the evidence—and if he can avoid throwing up in the process, all the better.

"It looks like dog poop," Mr. Castro states simply, looking back into the living room with the same funny look on his face. Meanwhile, his mountain-size dog is barking behind the fence like a crazy seal at feeding time.

"Aren't you the Sherlock boy?" he asks while squinting his eyes. "Uh, I don't get the joke, but we're watching a real good show about flying squirrels right now. Are you selling these photos to raise money or something?"

"Someone's dog left that on Mrs. Fefferland's lawn," I inform him, thinking about how fantastic that flying squirrel show must be since half the world seems to be

THE FLYING SQUIRREL

watching it. I get to the point quickly. "Could that be Ranger's poop, Mr. Castro?"

"Kid, Ranger sneezes things bigger than this," he laughs, handing back the photo. "Ranger weighs over two hundred and thirty pounds. Try looking for a beaver or a pigeon," he says, and closes the door with a loud thump.

"A beaver?" I say to nobody. "We don't have beavers around

here. And a pigeon dropping poops this size would have to be as big as a microwave oven."

My second official case is certainly off to a slow start.

I sit on the curb and pull out my list of suspects. I've got way too many suspects if I plan to solve this mystery by dinner. I take out a pink Girl Chat Sleepover marker (which I also borrowed without asking) and cross out Ranger, Cujo (too big), and the ancient Vader (too old). "That leaves just four suspects," I say—just as someone crashes a speeding truck through the Castros' fence.

I jump to my feet and look over my shoulder. With a combination of relief and utter panic, I realize that there's no truck crashing through the fence behind me. It's Ranger! His beach-ball-size head and his ham-sandwich-size paws are hanging over the fence . . . and the rest of him is working like mad to get over that fence, too!

I never find out if he makes it, because

I'm four houses away before I even start screaming.

This may not be the bravest way for a detective to act, but when you're about to become a moist and meaty doggie treat, there are few options. For a moment, I imagine all that would be left of me: my right shoe, my list of suspects, and a suspicious-looking pink Girl Chat Sleepover pen.

As I huff and puff along, I think for a moment that I might be a better sprinter than detective . . . but then I calculate that this unusual burst of speed is eighty-seven percent pure fear, twelve percent hunger for a solution to this mystery, and five percent desire to eat several helpings of my mom's spaghetti for dinner.

I finally run out of gas on the front lawn of the Moriartys' house. This is no accident. If I go any farther, I will surely start barfing up the seven frozen waffles I ate for breakfast. Also, Mr. and Mrs. Moriarty just happen to be the owners of Peekaboo, one of the remaining suspects on my list.

After what seems like fifty-three minutes, my breathing returns to normal, and I wobble up the steps to the Moriartys' front door.

Mr. and Mrs. Moriarty are a strange couple—they're friendly, neat, and always very polite. They're also often gone for weeks at a time. This gives the neighborhood gossips plenty to whisper and *tsk-tsk* about.

Lance has a theory that the Moriartys are aliens from the planet Uranus who visit Earth every few weeks to check out what's on TV.

My theory, on the other hand, is that Lance

just loves saying Uranus, and he'll say it any chance he gets. Everybody in our class at school thinks Lance is the funniest thing since sliced bread. His best jokes include saying Uranus all the time, making loud fart noises when it's real quiet, and playing "The Star-Spangled Banner" with his armpit. And when he's really on a roll, he can burp the alphabet all the way to the letter *R*. Ha, ha, ha. I can be pretty funny, too, but my best jokes usually aren't heard because of all the armpit racket.

Anyway, before I reach the door, Peekaboo starts barking like some pocket-size killer. I stand there shaking my head. This dog must be kidding! It's no bigger than a forty-two-ounce can of soup and looks like it will fall apart if you look at it funny. Match Peekaboo up against a salamander, and I'd bet on the lizard.

"Quiet, Peekaboo! Relax, boy, or your eyes are gonna bounce across that floor like marbles!" I scream through the door.

Maybe I shouldn't have used his name, because this seems to make Peekaboo go even more wild. Maybe Mr. and Mrs. Moriarty left town weeks ago without leaving any food for their soup-size pet. Maybe the dog's eyes have already popped out, and that's causing the barkathon. Maybe Peekaboo is being attacked by a mouse that's bigger than he is.

Whatever the reason, two things are clear: The Moriartys are not at home, and their home security system is dangerously close to losing its eyesight.

"Sorry, Peekaboo," I shout through the door. "I'll be going now." As I back away from the door and marvel at the thunderous yelping, I wonder if a boy my age might go to jail for blinding a neighbor's pet.

But my worries of a long prison sentence are interrupted by a deep voice coming from behind me—

"Don't move a muscle, Sherlock, or this dog *will* attack for sure."

· Chapter Ten ·
A Man's Best Friend?

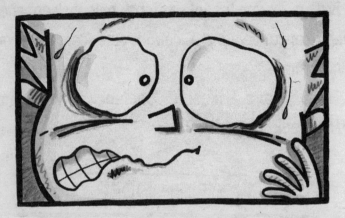

Preparing for the worst, my butt tenses up so much that I'm sure it would crack a walnut.

If there's anything more terrifying in the world than waiting for a dog to bite you in the behind, I don't know what it is. I've heard that when you get really terrified, your blood turns ice-cold, but I don't feel that way. I feel more like my brain has slipped down into my body and gotten stuck somewhere between my lungs and my bladder.

I can't think. I can't run. And, I'm sorry to say, I even let out a little squeak of fear.

Then I hear an odd snorting sound. When I whip my head around, ready to meet Ranger's fangs up close and personal, I find myself facing . . . Lance! Just Lance, standing there and laughing in a fake, deep voice.

"Where's the dog?" I squeak again, looking around wildly.

"I was just kidding," Lance says, shaking his head.

"Don't ever do that again!" I snap.

"Okay! Okay! Don't be so sensitive, Shirley," he snorts.

"My second case has gone from bad to badder!" I shout. "And now it's gone from worse to worser!"

"Hey, Sherlock, forget your dumb case. Let's go play some games at your house," he says.

"I thought you were going to play *Vengeance in Venice!* at your house after your grandma finished watching her super squirrels," I say, trying to catch my breath.

"Well, that was the plan," he mumbles. "But the next show was about three-legged bullfrogs, and my grandma got all interested. So here I am with my best game and nowhere to play it." He pulls the game out of his backpack to prove his point.

If you haven't already guessed, the only thing Lance likes to do more than watch TV is to play his *Vengeance in Venice!* video game. In the game, you basically run around in this flooded city and hop from canoe to canoe trying to catch an evil frog and save the city  from drowning. No matter how hard I try, I always fall into the putrid water and get eaten alive by a giant shellfish named Bernie. Lance loves *Vengeance in Venice!* because nobody can beat him, but I think all that game playing is making him "a bit daffy."

"Forget that game and come help me with my case," I plead. "I get ten bucks for solving it, and I'll give you half."

"That's sounds like a lot of knocking on doors, jumping fences, and snooping around for clues, so I don't think so," he says, putting on his backpack. "Sounds sort of boring."

"What? C'mon, Lance, I could use some help," I beg.

"Maybe tomorrow," he says over his shoulder as he heads back to his house.

"Hurry, or you'll miss the show about the North American yellow-bellied spineless chicken!" I call after him, but I don't think he hears me.

One thing is for sure. Detective work can give you a headache. And it was about to get a whole lot more painful.

"Sherlock, Mrs. Fefferland is on the phone," my mom informs me as I open the front door.

"Hello, Mrs. Fefferland," I say, taking the phone from my mom.

"Sorry to wake you from your nap, Mr. Rip Van Winkle!" she wheezes and clacks on the other end of the line.

"Nap?" I say. "What nap?"

"While you've been snoring in your cozy

bed, another steaming pile of dog evidence
has been planted on my lovely lawn," she
huffs.

"I-I wasn't sleeping," I sputter as I pull
out my list of suspects. "I've been eliminating suspects."

"While you've been eliminating suspects,
the real culprit has been eliminating on my
lawn," she grumbles. "I'm not very satisfied
with the results so far."

"Sorry, Mrs. Fefferland," I say. "I'll catch
this mutt before my mom serves dinner. Next
I plan to—"

"Now that's more like it, Sherlock," she
says, and hangs up on me.

"Uh . . . thank you, Mrs. Fefferland," I say
into the dead phone, so my mom doesn't know
Mrs. Fefferland hung up on me. "I'll see you
later. Bye."

I don't remember anyone ever hanging up on

Sherlock Holmes in any of his movies. But I guess they didn't have phones back then. His old maid was always bringing him little notes on a silver tray. Maybe I need a maid.

Already I've stepped in fresh dog poop, been ignored by my family, and almost been eaten by a three-hundred-pound dog—and I may have blinded a pocket-size pooch. Oh, and I've been scared out of my brain by my best friend.

Sherlock Holmes would have run home crying by now. But not me. I'm as stubborn as a zebra. And I still need to earn my stripes as a detective— especially if I ever want to get myself a maid with a silver tray.

"I'm ready, boss," my little sister says, suddenly entering the room. She's wearing safety goggles, a swimming cap, a raincoat, rubber boots, and yellow dishwashing gloves. "If we find any more poopy evidence, I'll collect the samples. You just watch my back. Now let's hit the streets!"

"You watch too much TV," I sigh. This case is turning into a stinker.

In just about every detective movie ever made, there's always a stakeout scene. Here's what happens on a stakeout: Two guys sit for hours in a car, drinking coffee and scarfing down tons of raspberry donuts. They usually just sit there getting to know each other better. They keep scarfing donuts until they're ready to barf their guts out. Then they suddenly sit up, spill their coffee all over the place, and follow a suspicious-looking guy who has just emerged from hiding in a suspicious-looking apartment.

I have a few problems with the basic stake-out concept. One: I don't drink coffee (it smells like burning hair). Two: I don't have any money to buy donuts. Three: I don't have a car to sit in while I stuff my face with gross coffee and expensive jelly-filled donuts. So, with no money, no car, and no donuts, I'm forced to do the best I can as a detective on his second official case. . . . I slowly starve behind Mrs. Fefferland's neatly trimmed hedges. Even worse, the only person I have to talk to is my little sister.

"This is more boring than Grandma's house," Hailey groans.

Ever notice how often detectives in movies bring a little sister along during a stakeout? The answer is NEVER! Now I know why.

"Did you ever notice that your nostrils are too big for your face?" she asks. I just ignore her.

"I can wiggle my ears!" she says. "Sherlock, look at my ears. Seriously."

"Would you be quiet?" I plead.

Hailey squirms and fidgets and sighs loudly several times. "Okay," she whispers, "I'm thinking of a number somewhere between zero and infinity. . . . Guess what it is."

I hold my head in my hands and moan.

"You'll never guess anyway," she says.

"The number is three hundred twelve. Math has never been your best subject."

"I can count one pain in the neck," I murmur. A few moments pass in magnificent silence. We both stare out at the lawn.

"Can you make bubbles with your spit?" she asks.

That's one thing about the great Sherlock Holmes: He never had to bring his irritating little sister along. I think that's why he solved so many dang cases—nobody was messing with his razor-sharp concentration skills.

"My leg is asleep," she whines. "And I think my left butt is, too!"

"Hailey, you're driving me bonkers!" I explode. "Just go home and get us something to eat! I'm so hungry, I can't rub two thoughts together."

"You might have to carry me," she gasps as she struggles to her feet. After tottering around in circles a few times on her sleeping leg and left butt, she limps off, shouting, "Good luck on the secret stakeout, Sherlock!"

Now that everybody in the country knows where I'm hiding for my stakeout, I decide to move. Sadly, the stakeout spot I choose next is the worst decision I've made in my nine and a half years of life on this earth.

At first I think my legs are falling asleep like Hailey's. But no matter which way I fold them, my legs still feel way weird. It's dark in the shadows under the stinky bush where I'm hiding, so it takes a few minutes for my eyes to adjust and confirm my worst fear: My pants have come to life!

I blink hard and look again. Sure enough, my pants are moving and my legs are not.

"Aaaaaaagh!" I shriek, slapping at my pants like they've burst into flames. I jump out of the bush and see that my pants are covered with ants. Thousands of ants. Million of ants. Grillions of ants! Then I freeze in terror. . . . They're IN MY PANTS, too!!!

I should point out here that I get totally freaked out by ants. I've been this way since I chose to sleep with my ant farm one night when I couldn't find my favorite teddy bear, Hank the Humming Bear. During the middle of the night, I woke up covered with ants and ran screaming right into my closet, where I cracked my head open on the bar you're supposed to hang your clothes on. Thirteen stitches later, my dad vacuumed up my ant farm, and we haven't discussed the incident since. So you can see how I might be a little touchy about the whole ants-in-my-pants business.

The next few minutes are a blur. But I fall onto Mrs. Fefferland's driveway and rip off my pants just as Mr. Fefferland turns into his driveway after a long trip to Singapore. Somehow I manage to stop screaming in terror long enough to wave hello.

Mr. Fefferland seems to take the whole wacko scene in stride.

"Is everything all right, Sherlock?" he asks as he steps out of his car with his trusty briefcase in hand. Nothing like returning from a business trip to find a wild-eyed kid in your driveway with no pants on.

"It's sort of a long story," I croak. "I'm working for your wife."

"I see," he says slowly. "Does she pay you a lot for this sort of thing?"

He asks this like he's in some kind of business meeting. I'm not sure how to respond because I've never been to a business meeting.

"I was helping her out with her poop problem," I stutter.

"I wasn't aware she had one," he replies. "And is this dance of yours helping her with her pooping?"

Even in my panic, I know that this is not going well. To make matters worse, I'm wearing my Inspector Wink-Wink underwear.

Inspector Wink-Wink was my favorite detective in the first grade, and I watched his cartoon show every chance I got. I even had cool Inspector Wink-Wink bedsheets until my sister washed them in her Girl Chat Sleepover washing machine and turned them flamingo pink.

So there I am, a fourth grader wearing goofy little-kid underwear, standing in my neighbor's driveway, breaking the bad news about his wife's poop problem. If my life were a TV show, this would be a great time to go to a commercial.

"I'll go and get some pants without ants!" I shout, hurrying down the driveway like some kind of pantless lunatic. "I'll be back to explain later."

"I can't wait to hear it," Mr. Fefferland calls after me.

As if this whole episode isn't bad enough, I'm sprinting back to a house that's been locked tight from the inside by its unofficial gatekeeper. I don't know it yet, but I'm about to cross paths with my always-annoyed, eye-rolling, brother-bugging big sister, Jessie.

• Chapter Fourteen •
Fort Sherlock and the Wicked Gatekeepers

"Jessie, open up!" I demand while standing on the welcome mat in my Inspector Wink-Wink briefs.

"Whatever it is you're selling, we don't want it," I hear her say from behind the door, and then laugh with my little sister like twin hyenas.

One of Jessie's most favorite hobbies is locking me out of the house. If it were 190 degrees outside and I were dying of thirst, she would lock me out of the house and think it was the funniest thing ever to happen on Earth since a hairy caveman somewhere in France discovered the practical joke.

I press the doorbell over and over, even though it broke several months ago. I'm sure my dad will get around to fixing it right after he mows our overgrown lawn.

"You'll be sorry," I threaten, but this just makes them laugh harder.

I jump back when the door's mail slot squeaks open and a sandwich slides through and drops onto the welcome mat. At least my assistant remembered to get me something to eat! I snatch up the sandwich and peel back the top slice of bread. Peanut butter. "Wha'?" I say stupidly. "Hailey, you know I'm allergic to peanut butter!" I shout at the peephole. The howling laughter that erupts from behind the door is so thunderous, I think they might pass out from lack of oxygen.

I rest my forehead on the cool door and think of the utter inconvenience of a peanut allergy. I'm sure the great Sherlock Holmes never had to worry about his head swelling up like a hot-air balloon if he ate a peanut. I'm even more allergic to bee stings. In fact, if I ever got stung by a bee while eating a peanut-butter sandwich, I would surely explode.

It's at a time like this that you wonder what life would be like with brothers instead of annoying sisters. " "Probably pretty dang normal," I mumble to myself.

Sometimes I imagine that I have two brothers, with real tough names like Shane and Buck. They teach me how to chop wood, track wild boars through the woods, and spit really far. I imagine that me and my two brothers dress like cowboys and rid our neighborhood of crime and bullies. We hold Olympic-style games in our backyard and improve our athletic abilities to almost genius levels. We build an air-conditioned tree house that—

"Hi, Sherlock," a voice suddenly says from behind me.

For the first time ever, my blood really does turn cold. Ice-water cold. Antarctica cold. No matter how bad life gets for me in the future, this will be one of the true low points. Why? This giggled greeting came from Sharon Sheldon, the smartest kid in my class and probably the most popular girl in our whole entire school.

"I'm sort of busy, Sharon," I say without turning around to face her.

"Yeah, it looks like it," she snickers. "Did you lose your house keys when you lost your pants?"

"What pants?" I say, as if it's perfectly normal to stand on your welcome mat in your underwear.

"Or are you trying to unlock that door with your sandwich?" she asks, really enjoying herself now.

I wish this day could start all over again.

"That's not Inspector Wink-Wink underwear, is it?" she says quietly.

On second thought, perhaps I should start my entire *life* over again.

At this point, I still haven't turned around, and you would think someone as smart and popular as Sharon Sheldon would get the hint that I don't feel like casual chitchat at the moment.

"Uh," I say, like some sort of underwear-wearing Frankenstein. "Uh, I'm on a case—"

"My brother loves you!" screeches Hailey through the mail slot. She screams this so loud, I almost lose my breath. "Sherlock wants to marry you!" comes another mail-slot screech. More laughing and giggling from the other side of the door. I will never be able to leave the house again.

"That's just my dopey sisters," I say, spinning around quickly. But Sharon Sheldon is gone. She's vanished. There's no trace of her. She has probably ridden off on her bike to report a hot story for tomorrow's gossip column in the *Baskerville Daily News*.

That's when I remember a forgotten doorway into our house that I'm sure my sisters have forgotten to lock. There is no time to waste. I have a case to solve by dinner . . . and my legs are getting cold.

· Chapter Fifteen ·
The Human Cork

My grandmother once told me that my most distinguishing feature is my fat head. My uncle Mycroft likes to say that in an emergency my head could be used as a flotation device. Even Miss Piffle complains that I have an abnormally thick skull.

I, on the other hand, have always thought my uncanny ability to solve mysteries was the result of a freakishly large brain.

Either way, my super-size noggin weighs heavily on my mind as I run up to Elvis's old doggie door.

We once had a family dog named Elvis. Don't ask why he was named Elvis—it wasn't my idea.

I still remember that every single time Elvis went out his doggie door, my dad would call out to nobody, "Elvis has left the building!" Elvis eventually ran away a few months ago and left our building for good—probably because all the "talking to plants" business started to give him the creeps, too.

I enter Elvis's door feetfirst instead of headfirst. I figure that by the time I have to squeeze my head through, I'll have momentum on my side and the rest of my body will somehow pull my head through.

I am terribly wrong.

I become stuck just as my armpits squeeze

through the tiny door. When I give up trying to squeeze in, I try to go back out. I squirm. I buck. I thrash. Still, I'm jammed into Elvis's doggie door like a hearing aid in an old guy's ear.

Then—in total desperation—I try panic. But even kicking and flopping around like a fish on the carpet doesn't do the trick. I'm stuck good, and my armpits hurt like crazy.

I try to calm down and imagine what the great Sherlock Holmes would do if he were in this situation. But I quickly realize that

he wasn't stupid enough to get himself trapped in a swinging doggie door without his pants on.

"Hey, Sherlock, I talked to Coach Lowney today," I hear my dad announce from inside the house.

"Uh . . . great," I wheeze.

"He says he saw you running down the street today like your life depended on it," he says from his side of the door.

"He's right about that," I gasp, wriggling like a dying worm on a hook.

"He thinks you've got the kind of natural speed you can't teach," he says.

"Certain death is a great motivator," I say.

"That's not Inspector Wink-Wink underwear, is it?" he asks.

"Dad! Hello! News flash! I'm stuck in a door here!" I shout.

"So I signed you up for Coach Lowney's

track and field team," he says casually, ignoring my cries for help.

"Dad, all I'm running right now is late," I simmer. "And this door is sure to slow me down at my first track meet, so could you please get me out of here?"

"Oh, no, you're becoming unhinged," he laughs. "Get it?"

"Nothing is funny when you're being eaten by a door," I rasp.

Twenty minutes and half a bottle of olive oil later, I slip out of Elvis's door and onto our back patio like some kind of greasy newborn pony.

"Sherlock has left the building!" I hear my dad holler from inside.

My sister Hailey has used up all her film recording my rescue on her Girl Chat Sleepover instant camera. "Where's the family photo album?" she shouts to my mom, who's busy on the phone with a frantic fern owner. Hailey gives me a fake smile as she holds up her camera. "Sherlock, did you know borrowing without asking is also known as stealing?"

My weird brother's butt

"Maybe we can find Sharon Sheldon's address in the phone book and send her one of these cute candid shots," Jessie says with a cackle as I stagger past her.

I give Jessie and Hailey my double-dare, gamma-ray, stink-eye glare.

"Thanks, Dad," I grumble, rubbing the olive oil into my red armpits while still glaring at my sisters like some kind of crazy wild boar.

"Now I've got a mystery to solve and only an hour until dinner," I say, marching past my mother in my underwear and greasy skin.

• Chapter Sixteen •
Stand Back,
I'm Going to Blow!

Smokey
Looks Fishy!
Can jump over small buildings!

If I don't get cracking on this case, I'll be a grandfather by the time I actually get around to solving it.

I sit on my bed and quickly write out a new list of suspects. I cross out all the names of suspects I've ruled out, keeping only those I still have to investigate. Fred, Smokey, and Ted still remain as possible poopers. I cross off Peekaboo because he's busy barking his eyes out in maximum security while the Moriartys are out of town—or off the planet.

Smokey is the best suspect to start with. He gets out several times a week and is often seen roaming the neighborhood to the beat of his own drummer. There's just one problem: Smokey belongs to Sharon Sheldon's family.

The thought of knocking on Sharon Sheldon's door so soon after she's seen me in my Inspector Wink-Wink underwear makes me feel real barfy. But like any good detective, I decide I must do what's best to keep my investigation moving forward. I ask my mom to call Sharon's mom.

"Forget it," my mom says. "That woman is still upset about your volcano stunt."

This opens up a whole

other can of worms, so I'll just give you the short end of the stick. . . .

I was assigned one of those creepy group science projects a few months ago, with Lance and Sharon Sheldon on my project team. We decided to do a report about volcanoes. I was in charge of building a model volcano, Sharon Sheldon was to explain what happens during an eruption, and Lance was going to make loud volcano noises and stuff when I turned on the volcano.

Sadly, I did not know that our dog, Elvis, had chewed on some of the electrical wires the night before our presentation. So just as Sharon Sheldon was starting to give her introduction and Lance started to make low, rumbling noises with his armpit, my volcano's battery somehow melted, burst into flames, and burned a big, black, stinky hole straight through Miss Piffle's desk.

I didn't think it was such a big deal, but some of the firefighters said a few sparks had burned some holes in Sharon's shoes.

Mrs. Sheldon was still ticked off at me and my family for putting Sharon in danger, even though it was basically the wire-chewing Elvis who had almost burned the school to the ground, not me.

Just the idea of calling the Sheldon house makes me feel like I have hot molten lava swishing around in my stomach, all ready to come roaring out of my mouth just as I say hello. But as some famous guy once said, you gotta do what you gotta do. So I take a deep breath and dial.

• Chapter Seventeen •
The Sherman Tank

Hiding behind a wilting ficus tree in our living room, I listen to the phone ring once, then twice. Just as I become certain that right after the third ring I'm going to qualify for the Heaving Hall of Fame, the phone is suddenly answered.

"Hello?" blurts out Sherman Sheldon, Sharon's bulky older brother and the meanest sixth grader ever to walk the halls of

Baskerville Elementary.

"Is Sharon home?" I ask in a cleverly disguised voice.

"Great balls of fire!" Sherman Sheldon barks. "It's Sherlock, the human flamethrower! You want to burn our house down now, you little freak?"

"No, I just want to talk to Sharon real quick," I say, dropping the cleverly disguised voice.

"She's busy watching some disgusting show about frogs with extra legs," he says with a loud sniff.

"It's just a quick question about some poop I'm looking into," I reply.

"You're looking into poop?

You really are a twisted little freak!" he shouts. He drops the phone with a loud bang, and I can hear him walking down the hallway calling, "It's Volcano Boy for Sharon!"

"What does he want?" I hear Mrs. Sheldon hiss.

I decide right then and there that ten bucks is not worth all this.

"Hi, Sherlock," Sharon says after finally picking up the phone.

"Sorry to bother you during your three-legged frog show," I mumble.

"Whatever," she says.

Although she's the smartest kid in our class, Sharon Sheldon says "whatever" all the time. It's her favorite thing to say. I'm never sure whether it means "I don't have time to get into it with a creep like you" or "No big deal, so don't worry about it." Either way, I decide to get this over with before Mrs. Sheldon calls the fire marshal or I become a vomiting volcano.

"Sharon, Mrs. Fefferland asked me to find out whose dog has been pooping in her yard," I say quickly. "Do you think it could have been your dog?"

"Smokey?" she asks. "Well, my dad took Smokey with him a few days ago on a hunting trip."

"Oh," I say like a real genius. "Oh," I say again, just to sound extra brilliant. "That means that it couldn't have been Smokey. He's in the clear." I draw a line through Smokey's name on my list of suspects—I'm actually getting somewhere!

"Whatever," she says.

"Um, sorry about today," I say, staring up at the ceiling.

"Whatever," she says.

Whew! At least she's not making a big deal out of the underwear thing.

"I hope you find your pooper," she says.

"That's sick!" her brother screams in the background.

"Well, now my suspects have been narrowed down to just Ted and Fred."

"It's not Ted," she laughs. "The Martin family moved away last month."

"Really?" I say. "Nobody told me! That means it can only be—"

"And Fred just had puppies two days ago."

"WHAT?" I squeak like I'm choking to death on a harmonica. I gape in horror at my list of suspects. "How can a dog named Fred have puppies?"

"Fred is short for Frederica," she replies.

"Oh," I say quietly. "This is terrible . . . horrible . . . shocking news."

"Whatever," Sharon says. "Well, anyway, Sherlock, don't feel so bad. . . . I used to watch *Inspector Wink-Wink*, too."

"Whatever," I sigh, and gently hang up the phone.

I stare at the phone for what feels like 112 years.

I'm back where I started. I'm sunk. Sunk in deep doo-doo.

Worst of all, I'm all out of suspects, and we eat dinner in twenty minutes.

Chapter Eighteen

When the Going Gets Tough, Consider Quitting

After all I have been through, I have to admit I still have no idea who is pooping on Mrs. Fefferland's lovely, carpetlike lawn. I need a break in the case, and I need it fast.

I walk down the hall to my room like a zombie. The smell of olive oil floats up off my ribs and armpits and reminds me just how hungry I am. I plop down at my desk and write out everything I've discovered so far.

This does not take very long. In fact, it barely takes eight seconds.

In every detective movie, the main guy always goes back over the evidence he's collected and looks for something he's missed. A little scrap of overlooked evidence. A small fact that doesn't add up. A clue that gets filed in the wrong drawer. Usually by the time he starts drooling and looking like a werewolf because he hasn't shaved in seven and a half days, he stumbles across the missing clue, sits up straight, and shouts, "How could I have been so stupid?"

Me, on the other hand? I just sit at my desk and mutter, "How could I have been stupid enough to take this dumb case?"

I review my three instant photos of mystery dog poop, my poop map, and my list of suspect poopers. I have to face facts: I'm pooped out.

"I heard Mrs. Fefferland hung up on you."

It's Hailey. She's poking her head into my room. Like most little sisters, Hailey can always sense when I want to be alone, and within seconds she moves just close enough to become the fly in my mental ointment. "Who told you that?" I ask without looking at her.

"Mom told me," she says, moving casually over to my desk. "She's says you tried to trick her and kept talking on the phone, but it didn't work."

"Can I help you?" I ask, trying my best to roll my eyes like Jessie.

"I also heard Mrs. Sheldon thinks you tried to blow up her daughter," she says, picking up my Inspector Wink-Wink pencil sharpener and turning it over in her hands.

"Hey, that's a rare collector's item," I say,

plucking the pencil sharpener from her hands.

"Touchy!" she says as if she's totally unaware that she's making me crazy. "Dad says he signed you up for Coach Lowney's track and field team because he's afraid you're becoming weird."

"No!" I snap. "It was Coach Lowney's idea. He thinks I have the kind of natural speed you can't teach."

"Apparently you're a lot better at running than solving mysteries," she says, studying my face through one of my magnifying glasses. "You might want to get those nostrils looked at by a doctor."

I grab the magnifying glass out of her hand.

"Hailey, I finally got my second official case as a detective, and it's not going so splendid! So if you have nothing nice to say, don't say anything at all."

She's silent as she thinks about this for a moment. "Sorry about that peanut-butter sandwich thing. And for telling Sharon Sheldon that you love her. And for taking your picture while you were stuck in the door in your underpants."

"You've been a great help," I say, rubbing my forehead in my palms as I review all the mistakes I've made today.

I consider knocking on Mrs. Fefferland's door and calling the whole thing off. I consider heading over to Lance's house for a quick game of *Vengeance in Venice!* I even consider hanging up my magnifying glass for good.

"Remember who taught you your times tables?" Hailey asks, picking up my poop map.

"You did," I moan, certain that this line of

questioning will have no point other than to make me irritated and miserable.

"And who taught you the names of all the planets?" she asks.

"You did," I sigh.

"And who taught you the names of all the state capitals?" she asks.

"You did," I reply, "but I've forgotten most of those."

"That's exactly my point," she says.

I slump in my chair. "You mean this little pep talk of yours actually has a point?"

"Look, Sherlock, I'm good at some things and you're good at other things," she says, pointing at me with my poop map. "I'm good at things that require complicated brain functions, like math and spelling and memorizing things and acting normal. You're good at creative problem solving and using your imagination to try out crazy theories in your head.

You also have a rare talent for getting your-self stuck in doors and other goofy situations that I would never even think of."

"You just had to add that last part, didn't you?" I say, shaking my head.

"Just don't get all crabby and frustrated," she says, walking toward the door. "You'll figure it out. You always do."

"Where are you going?" I ask.

"I'm watching this show about frogs with too many legs and I just came in here to entertain myself during a commercial," she says, closing my door slowly. "And Mom wanted me to tell you that we're eating dinner in fifteen minutes."

"Some assistant you are," I grumble.

"Hey, if you end up a complete failure as a detective, you can always use all that natural speed as a pizza delivery boy," she giggles, slamming the door before I can say anything else.

I wonder if everyone's little sister has to get the last word in. But she's right. I always seem to manage to solve things one way or another. I'll get to the bottom of Mrs. Fefferland's poop. I just need a little luck.

Then I get the lucky break I've been waiting for all day.

• Chapter Nineteen •
The Tip of the Iceberg?

In detective shows on TV, the main guy sometimes has to admit that he is powerless to solve his case. And just as he plucks his worn-out jacket off the back of the chair to head home for a long weekend of stewing in his own horribleness, he gets a phone call that cracks the case open like a stubborn jaw-breaker.

At first, the caller on the phone sounds like

just another wack job, some crazy nut trying to drive the detective bonkers. But then, with his eyes bulging out of his head like big, hard-boiled eggs, the detective realizes that this is the tip he's been waiting for. The music gets really loud at this point and the detective explodes out the door to solve the case.

My hot tip—like all traditional hot tips you see on TV—comes from the last person on Earth you'd expect to call you with a hot tip.

"Hello," I say, taking the phone from my mom as I enter the kitchen.

The smell of bubbling spaghetti sauce is now so powerful that my knees almost buckle. Since I'm so hungry and could easily faint and split my head open on a chair or something, I stumble into the jungle that was once our living room.

"Sherlock, it's me, Lance!" my best friend's voice booms from the phone.

"I can't play video games right now," I say.

"Sherlock, I've got your mystery solved!" he announces.

"What are you talking about?" I yelp.

"I just saw a dog running loose in the neighborhood," he says, "and it looks like a pooping machine."

"How does a dog look like a pooping machine?" I shout.

"I don't know," he replies. "But it looked like it was up to no good. Something about the tail looked extra creepy."

"Whose dog is it? Where is it now?" I roar into the phone, forgetting my rumbling stomach for a moment.

"I'm not sure whose dog it is, but it's heading your way!" he says.

"Go out and catch it for me and I'll be there in thirty seconds!" I say.

"That's impossible," he says. "I've got to watch this show with my grandma about these frogs with three legs—"

I hang up, grunt in frustration, and race out the door at a full sprint. Finally it's time to meet my mystery pooper face-to-face.

"We're eating dinner in ten minutes!" my mom calls after me just before the screen door bangs shut.

My stomach growls back like a confused gorilla in a cardboard box.

• Chapter Twenty •
Run, Joe, Run!

Lance lives down the street and around the corner from me. My fastest-ever time to his house was thirty-seven seconds, but today I feel like I could make it in thirty seconds flat.

My teacher, Miss Piffle, once told us about some ancient Roman hero guy named Mercury who was as fast as anything. Of course, all the Roman people went all nuts over him 'cause he was so speedy and terrific. Well, in our workbook there's a picture of this Mercury guy, and he's got little wings growing out of his head and his ankles! Who couldn't be fast if they had a couple of extra wings, right? That's practically cheating. That's like bragging about how much pizza you can eat when your mouth just happens to be as big as a sofa. Anyway, today I think I could even take that Mercury guy in a race, even with buffalo wings on his temples and smelly feet.

As I'm daydreaming about beating the pants off this Mercury guy, Coach Lowney drives past.

"Keep it up, Sherlock!" he howls, leaning out of his car window. "You look like the next state champion!"

State champion? Now, I like the sound of that. Running on the track team sure sounds a lot more glamorous than solving poopy little mysteries.

As I zoom down the street, I start thinking of nicknames I might try for my career as a track star: The Speed Freak. Hot Socks. Thunder Pants. Maybe, I think for a brief moment, the Boy With Some Serious Gas.

Sure, these names will need some fine-tuning, but I'm on to something. I decide right then and there that when it comes to running on Coach Lowney's track team, I'll let my legs do the talking. And they are about to start screaming. . . .

Because coming at me in full attack mode from the other direction is not a dog that looks like a pooping machine, but Cujo, the Ashers' new dog, and he looks a lot more like a kid-eating machine!

As I turn and run for my life, I make a quick mental note to strangle my best friend, Lance.

• Chapter Twenty-one •
Animal Instincts

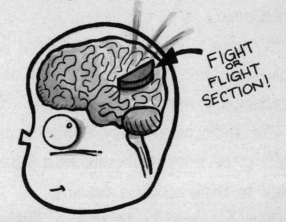

FIGHT
OR
FLIGHT
SECTION!

My dad once told me that there's a section of a person's brain about the size of a hockey puck that controls our animal instincts. Basically, it's the chunk of brain that helped the first humans survive in the world before we invented things like frozen burritos and cable TV. "This section controls your 'fight or flight' response," he said, tapping the back of my head. "It's the only part of the brain we humans have in common with donkeys and ferrets and other animals of that ilk."

I had no idea what he was talking about. Until now.

My brain's hockey puck is now in full flight mode, and my legs are pumping as fast as hummingbird wings.

The fight part of my hockey puck doesn't seem to be working, because all I can get my brain to think about is running.

Cujo has quickly become a legend in my neighborhood. Once Sherman Sheldon told me a mailman mysteriously disappeared without a trace one day, right after delivering the Ashers' mail. The snarling I hear from behind me makes me believe that story more than ever.

For a second I think I can even smell Cujo's breath—which smells weirdly like my dad's burps after he eats too much candied-yam casserole.

Bottom line: Cujo is closing in fast.

Could the odor of olive oil on my skin be causing a feeding frenzy?

I'm too far from my house to make it safely there (and my sisters would probably lock me out anyway). Lance's house is in the opposite direction. So I try diversion.

I cut onto the Castros' lawn and run through their sprinklers. I jump over several neatly trimmed hedges. I even knock over a big stone birdbath by accident, but Cujo is still at my heels.

In front of me I see Mrs. Fefferland's white picket fence. It just might provide some protection. I have nothing to lose . . . but my legs and my arms!

So I make the leap of my life, spin around, and through the slats of that fence I see that Cujo is just three feet from me and moving in fast for the kill.

· Chapter Twenty-two ·
Alarm Bells

Have you ever watched one of those nature shows where some crazy guy is underwater in a cage and a giant shark is rocketing straight at him with his jaw open and all 364 razor-sharp teeth ready for business?

That's all I can think of as I wait for my life to flash before my eyes. But it never does . . .

Because Cujo just runs on by.

He doesn't burst through the fence and snatch me up like a rag doll. He doesn't snarl and gnash his big teeth. He doesn't even look at me.

He's just gone. There is just a faint whiff of candied-yam casserole in the air. Nothing more.

My heart is banging around in my chest like a cat in a paper bag. But I'm safe. I'm all in one piece.

So why do I hear alarm bells? Did someone call the police? Is a fire truck rolling down the street to come to my rescue?

I realize the clanging is just my mom's dinner bell. Even after my near-death experience, I still find that bell irritating.

When dinner is ready, my mom always walks out onto our porch and rings this big cowbell so me and my sisters will come and eat. But she rings that dang thing even when we're already sitting at the table. She says it was a tradition on her family's farm when she was growing up. On a farm, a cowbell calling you for dinner is no big deal. But in a neighborhood with kids like Sherman Sheldon around, you might as well wear a sign that says I'M A MAJOR DOOFUS. PLEASE KICK ME HARD ON MY BACKSIDE.

"Between that cowbell and all that talking to plants," Lance told me one day, "your mom just might be loony."

I stand uneasily on my now-rubbery legs and steady myself against Mrs. Fefferland's fence. This had been some day. In any detective's notebook, I figure that this day would be marked down as a complete and total and utter disaster without any—

That's when I hear it . . . a creepy scratching noise that makes the hairs on the back of my neck stand straight up.

I spin around in terror. There's nobody there. Just that spooky scratching noise that sounds like it's coming from another world.

And that's when it hits me: Maybe the poops covering Mrs. Fefferland's lawn have been planted by Elvis's ghost!

My old dog has returned to haunt my neighborhood!

CUJO

Meat eater!
Note: bring treats. Big treats!!!

• Chapter Twenty-three •
The Ghost Appears

When I see the white shape float silently onto the lawn in the dim evening light, my heart stops beating.

My brain's hockey puck does a backflip.

My body prepares to launch a scream so loud that it will set off car alarms for several blocks.

But then the scream gets caught in my throat.

As the white ghost trots across the lawn and starts spinning in preparation for what dogs like to do on lawns, I realize that I'm not looking at Elvis's ghost at all . . . I'm looking at Mrs. Fefferland's dog, Tinker.

"What the—," I gurgle. I stagger back a few steps and blink, trying to grasp exactly what this means. It's as if the computer in my mind has crashed and I'm waiting for it to reboot.

I look back over my shoulder to confirm that the gate is closed. It is. My eyes scan the entire length of the fence for any openings that I've previously overlooked. There are none. "Mrs. Fefferland?" I call out in a high-pitched voice that I don't even recognize as my own. There is no answer.

At this point my head begins to spin and my vision becomes a blurry mix of white picket fence, lovely green grass, and swirling dog poops.

Suddenly, in a remote area at the back of my brain, a small connection is made. I'm rebooting. My head stops spinning. Something clicks into place.

I take several carefully placed hops across the lawn and over to the fence. Somehow I know what I'm looking for. Then I find it! In the darkening shadows behind the bushes is the entrance to a small tunnel. Of course! The scratching noise I just heard was actually Tinker coming through a tunnel. Tinker has a secret tunnel that runs from Mrs. Fefferland's backyard, under the fence, and directly into the gated front yard!

I watch as Tinker finishes her business, scampers past me, and slips back down into her secret tunnel. She disappears down the hole and returns to Mrs. Fefferland's backyard.

The tunnel is not more than three feet from where I sat a few hours before and got

covered with ants during my stakeout. I'm not sure if this fact makes me want to laugh or cry, and for a moment I teeter on the edge of both.

Finally I laugh. My case is solved. I've solved my second official case as a detective.

Mrs. Fefferland is more surprised than I am. She doesn't even believe me until I show her the tunnel myself.

She wheezes and clacks at her husband about getting a shovel out of the garage and plugging up Tinker's tunnel. She rumbles around in circles several times, clacking to herself, before she realizes I'm still there.

After Mr. Fefferland produces a ten-dollar

bill, Mrs. Fefferland wheezes good night, and then she asks me to keep this little incident between us.

I agree.

As I'm about to leave, Mr. Fefferland stops me. "Good work, Sherlock," he whispers with a chuckle and a wink. He quickly slips me another ten-dollar bill. "That's a tip for a job well done."

"Thanks a million," I say, carefully folding and pocketing my twenty bucks and running off to celebrate with a few heaping piles of spaghetti.

Looking back now, it seems like I should have figured out the Case of the Neighborhood Stink a lot earlier than I did. But as a kid still new to the detective game, I learned that every mystery has to run its own course. Because if you stick to it long enough, and keep your eye on the ball, the answer eventually falls right into your lap.

And if you're lucky, you'll be home in time for dinner.

Introducing Joe Sherlock, Kid Detective!

Case #000001:
The Haunted Toolshed
Hc 0-06-076189-X
Pb 0-06-076188-1

Case #000002:
The Neighborhood Stink
Hc 0-06-076187-3
Pb 0-06-076186-5

Case #000003:
The Missing Monkey-Eye Diamond
Hc 0-06-076191-1
Pb 0-06-076190-3

Joe Sherlock was born with a fear of the dark, an allergy to peanut butter, and a natural gift for solving mysteries.

Read all the books in the series and find out whether the weird, bizarre, and embarrassing will stump this great kid detective.